STIRLING COUNCIL LIBRARIES

3804802 029097 4

D1494447

Magic Pony

Seaside Detectives

The lodgers were right outside. Natty grabbed the bedspread and flung it back over the workbench.

"Get on," said Ned, but there was no time. Instead Natty raced across the barn and wriggled between some straw bales just as the doors were pulled open while Ned went from big to small in a flash. The two brothers were silhouetted against the light and Natty hardly dared breathe in case she rustled the straw.

STIRLING LIBRARIES	
3804802 029097 4	
HJ	16-Jul-2009
	£5.99

Summer Special

Magic Pony

Seaside Detectives

Illustrated by Peter Kavanagh

■SCHOLASTIC

For Benedick Gibson, with love

Scholastic Children's Books
An imprint of Scholastic Ltd
Euston House, 24 Eversholt Street
London, NW1 1DB, UK
Registered office: Westfield Road, Southam, Warwickshire, CV47 0RA
SCHOLASTIC and associated logos are trademarks and/or registered
trademarks of Scholastic Inc.

First published in the UK by Scholastic Inc, 1999
This edition published in the UK by Scholastic Ltd, 2009

Text copyright © Elizabeth Lindsay, 1999
Illustrations copyright © Peter Kavanagh, 1999
The right of Elizabeth Lindsay and Peter Kavanagh to be identified as the
author and illustrator of this work has been asserted by them.

Cover illustration © Charlotte Macrae

ISBN 978 1407 10913 8

A CIP catalogue record for this book is available from the British Library

All rights reserved
This book is sold subject to the condition that it shall not, by way of trade or
otherwise, be lent, hired out or otherwise circulated in any form of binding or
cover other than that in which it is published. No part of this publication may
be reproduced, stored in a retrieval system, or transmitted in any form or by
any means (electronic,
mechanical, photocopying, recording or otherwise) without the prior
written permission of Scholastic Limited.

Printed in the UK by CPI Bookmarque, Croydon, Surrey
Papers used by Scholastic Children's Books are made from wood grown in
sustainable forests.

1 3 5 7 9 10 8 6 4 2

This is a work of fiction. Names, characters, places, incidents and dialogues are
products of the author's imagination or are used fictitiously. Any resemblance
to actual people, living or dead, events or locales is entirely coincidental.

www.scholastic.co.uk/zone

Contents

Chapter 1
The Journey

Natty marked the start of going on holiday from the moment she unpinned the poster of Ned, her special magic pony, from above her chest of drawers. She had been excited all through the hustle and bustle of getting packed and driving to the station. Yet the thrill of setting out had ebbed away once she was sitting on the train. Fields and hedges, trees and rivers came and went but the journey to the seaside was taking for ever.

With nothing to do but sit still, Natty was soon drowsy. Without her meaning them to, her eyelids closed, and she drifted into a far-away sleep, where a chestnut pony stepped into her dreams and came trotting across a sandy beach to stop by her side.

"Hello, Natty," the pony said.

"Ned," she cried, giving him a welcoming smile. "I'm so glad to see you!" She sprang into the saddle at

once, and her leggings and sweatshirt
disappeared, to be replaced by smart
riding clothes.

"Hold tight!" cried the pony, and they galloped away across the sands to where the pounding waves foamed and the salt spray flew.

"Fancy a swim?" the pony asked.

"But what about my magic riding clothes? They'll get wet."

"No they won't!" Looking down, Natty saw she was wearing her swimming-costume.

"Yes, I'd love a swim," she cried, holding tight to the pony's chestnut mane. "I'm hot after all that galloping."

The pony stepped into the foaming water and a giant wave

broke over them. Natty held her breath, expecting to splutter. When her eyes suddenly opened she found it wasn't a wave at all but Mum stroking her hair.

"Wake up, Natty. We've arrived."

"Arrived where?" she asked, quite forgetting she was in a train.

"What do you mean arrived where?" snorted Jamie, in typical elder brother fashion. "At Westsands of course. You've been snoring!"

"Take no notice," said Dad. "You fell asleep, that's all."

After such a dream, Natty longed to ride on the beach in real life and was sure that she would. She was holding tight to a cardboard tube and rolled up inside was Ned's pony poster. It had been an unbearable thought that he might come out of his picture and turn into a real live pony while she was away. But now he was coming with her there was no chance of that. She had also packed Esmerelda, Prince and Percy, her three china ponies, who lay tucked up safely in her rucksack. She didn't want them to miss out on the fun either.

Jamie pushed past, almost knocking the cardboard tube from her hands.

"Watch out!" cried Natty.

"I can't think why you wanted to bring that soppy poster," he said.

"Mr Cosby sold it to you to go on the wall, not to take everywhere."

"You've brought your bike, I'm bringing my poster. OK!"

"Well, you can't ride a pony poster, can you?" said Jamie.

"No, I can't ride a pony poster! So what?" Natty longed to add – but I can ride a magic pony! But she didn't.

Ned was Natty's biggest secret. Sometimes he came out of the poster and turned into a real live pony, the same size as Penelope Potter's pony, Pebbles, who lived in the field opposite her home, and sometimes he magicked himself to the miniature size of Percy, the smallest of her china ponies.

Natty had bought Ned from Cosby's Magic Emporium, Jamie's favourite shop. Maybe Mr Cosby knew about Ned's magic or maybe he didn't. His eyes had certainly twinkled on that wonderful day when he had sold her the poster, but Ned had told her the magic was a secret and Natty had promised never to tell.

"Stop bickering, you two," said Dad. "And get a move on."

Natty picked up her rucksack and jumped on to the platform. She sniffed. The air was different at the seaside. It tasted salty.

"I want to see the sea," she cried, starting to run.

"You will, just wait for us," called Mum, but Natty couldn't wait. Now they had arrived she wanted to see the sea straight away.

Chapter 2
Westsands

Pedalling lazily, Jamie caught Natty up by the station entrance. "Dad says you're not to go on the road. You've got to wait."

"I won't go on the road," said Natty, but she didn't wait. She hurried by the taxi rank while the cry of a gull reminded her that somewhere near was a wide rolling ocean. She passed the Welcome to Westsands sign where the road ran downhill to the town and looked beyond the rooftops, to see, in the far-away distance, the sunlit sky meet the dark, deep green of the sea.

Jamie skidded to a halt beside her. "There, you've seen it now. Happy?"

He was hiding a grin and Natty knew that he was as excited as she was only he was trying not to show it. She clasped Ned's poster to her, glad she had brought it.

"How far to the holiday cottage?"

she asked.

"Don't know," said Jamie. "Dad's got the map. It's out of town so it must be quite a way. With luck it'll be up on the cliffs."

They were distracted by a squeal of brakes coming from a tatty green van which drew up sharply against the kerb, forcing Jamie to lift his bike on to the pavement. Two men climbed out and, from the back of the van, took some rolls of paper and a bucket.

In no time at all they were pasting up not one but four posters, on to the billboard next to the pavement, not seeming to care that they were putting them in the middle of a railway travel poster. Then, putting back the paste bucket, they drove off in a cloud of smelly exhaust fumes, leaving Natty and Jamie with nothing more than a scowl from the driver.

"Pooh!" said Natty. "That van must be nearly on fire."

Jamie was studying the four posters, each one the same as the others. Two men peered out, both with painted white faces. On their heads were black top hats and swirling about them was a storm of paper money.

"Listen to this!" he said. "At The Palace Theatre For One Sensational Night Only – The Stevenage Brothers Present – DOUBLE YOUR MONEY – The Magic Show You Cannot Afford To Miss."

"When is it?" Natty asked.

"The sixth of August at seven-thirty. That's tomorrow evening. We've got to go!" Jamie spun round on his bike.

"What does it mean – Double Your Money?" Natty asked.

"Dunno. Some sort of game, I expect. Just think, Natty, one day it could be me at the Palace Theatre.

And you. The Amazing Jamie Deakin and his assistant, Natalie."

Natty pulled a face. "No, it won't be me," she said. "I'll be too busy riding in horse shows. Penelope might be your assistant. I think she'd rather like to be."

"Penelope Potter! No thanks!" Jamie pulled a face. "I'd rather do the show on my own."

"Why does it say 'the magic show you cannot afford to miss'? It must be something to do with getting lots of money."

"I can't think how," said Jamie. "But I shan't miss it, that's for sure."

Natty laughed, knowing Jamie was too keen on conjuring to do that. Natty didn't want to miss it either. Not if you really could double your money.

Dad drew up beside them on his bike, which he'd brought to keep Jamie company.

"Hurry up, Natty. Mum's waiting for you in the taxi."

"Dad, there's a conjuring show tomorrow," said Jamie. "We want to go."

"Can we?" Natty asked.

Dad smiled. "I don't see why not."

Natty trotted back to the station

entrance, leaving Jamie and Dad to their cycling. Holding tight to Ned's cardboard tube, she clambered into the taxi.

"Where to?" asked the lady who was driving.

"Sea View Cottage," replied Mum. "It's off the Westsands Old Road."

"I know it," said the driver.

Jamie and Dad were free-wheeling down the hill into the town when the taxi drove by. Natty waved.

"This is the High Street," said the driver and at the traffic lights she turned right. "And this is the Sea Front."

A wide sandy bay stretched out in front of them with miles of sand running down to the sea. "The tide's out at the moment," said the taxi lady. "But, when it's in, the sea comes right up."

"What's that?" asked Natty, pointing to what looked like a giant bridge on stilts striding out into the water.

"The pier," said Mum. "Westsands is famous for its pier."

"And for the Palace Theatre," said the taxi driver. "Don't forget the good old Palace."

Natty could see that the pier grew wider at its sea end and there was

a huge domed building sitting high
above the water.

"Is that the Palace Theatre, right at the far end?"

"Yes, that's it."

"There's a magic show on tomorrow night, called Double Your Money."

"Double Your Money! Sounds like the magic show not to be missed."

"The thing is," Natty told the taxi driver, "my brother Jamie's a conjurer. He does really good tricks. That's why he wants to go to the magic show. I want to go to get rich."

"I don't think you should hold out too many hopes," said Mum, laughing.

"But why not? The show's called Double Your Money!" said Natty.

"Natty, even if you doubled all your money, you still wouldn't have enough to be rich."

"I'd have enough to buy twice as many ice-creams."

"That's true, I suppose," smiled Mum.

"Well, if it's ice-creams you're after, the best place to go is Bertollini's Ice-Cream Parlour. Mr Bertollini sells the tastiest ice-cream in Westsands. There's his shop now."

The taxi sped past the pier entrance and, opposite, Natty glimpsed tables on the pavement outside a shop hung with a huge pink and white awning.

"Yummy! I must go to the magic show. I do want to double my ice-cream money."

"Well, good luck to you, dearie," said the taxi lady, driving them out of town. "There's nothing like a bit of magic in your life."

Natty was sure that, inside the tube, Ned's poster wriggled in agreement. Smiling happily, she hugged it close.

With the sea spread out beside them the driver turned the car off the road on to a gravel track. "Sea View Cottage is up here and a fine sea view is what you get," she said, and the taxi drew up outside a white house with a grey slate roof.

By the time they had hauled the suitcases in through the front door Natty was puffed, but perked up when Mum let her choose the bedroom that faced out across the treetops to the glittering waves.

"There might be a storm," she cried, dropping Ned's poster and her rucksack on to the bed. "And a shipwreck."

"There might be," said Mum. "But if there's bad weather you won't be able to play on the beach or go swimming."

"I didn't think of that," said Natty, with a frown which disappeared the moment she heard the tinkling of bicycle bells. "They're here!" And racing downstairs and out into the garden she found Jamie and Dad, hot and red in the face from their hard ride up the hill from town.

"Phew," said Jamie, dropping his bike on the grass and collapsing beside it. "Am I thirsty!"

"I've found the kitchen," said Mum. "I'll bring you out some water."

"Isn't this lovely," said Natty. "And look, the track goes on to somewhere else and there's a path alongside the garden that leads towards the cliff. We must explore!"

"We will," said Dad, sitting on the step to get his breath back. "All in good time."

Leaving Jamie and Dad to recover, Natty bounded up the stairs to her sea view bedroom. Pulling off the plastic stopper, she gave a gentle pull to Ned's poster and slid it from its cardboard tube.

On one side of the window were some shelves and Natty weighted the top of the poster with some books and let it hang down over them. It curled a bit at the bottom but it meant Ned could look out to sea if he wanted.

"There, Ned," said Natty, pleased. "Welcome to Sea View Cottage."

Next she unpacked Esmerelda, Prince and Percy and lined up the china ponies on the window-sill, making the room feel just like home.

She pushed open the window. Below her was a garden and at the end of the garden was a small field.

Beyond the field a path lead into a wood of wind-bent trees which dropped away towards the sea. But there was no harsh wind today, just the hum of bees and a butterfly fluttering above the fence.

"Isn't it lovely, Ned?" sighed Natty but before she had a chance to say more there was a loud hee-haw honking. "What's that?" She jumped up alarmed as the hee-haw honking happened again and again. "Oh, I think I know!"

And leaving Ned's poster to flutter, Natty raced downstairs and out of the house to see if she was right.

Chapter 3
Meet Dora

The noise appeared to be coming from further along the track. Natty began to run.

"Hey, wait for me!" It was Jamie waving from his bedroom window. "I'm coming too."

Hee-haw, hee-haw, hee-haw, came the insistent cry.

"Then hurry up," cried Natty. "I want to get there before it stops."

Jamie raced down the garden path to join her. "What is it?"

"Something furry with floppy ears," guessed Natty.

"A rabbit!" Jamie teased.

"No, of course not a rabbit."

The pair of them pelted down the track. They rounded a corner where there was nothing to see except hedgerow before the track started uphill again. The hee-haw honking was loud and clear. Out of breath, Jamie slowed, but Natty hurried on round the bend.

The hee-haw honking stopped at once. In the silence that followed, Natty found herself walking across a weed-covered yard towards a tumble-down cottage with a bend in the roof. There was a notice pinned to the peeling paint on the door announcing Fresh Eggs For Sale.

Turning round, Natty discovered a shaggy grey face peering curiously at her over the top of a gate.

"I was right," she smiled as Jamie arrived on the scene. "It's a donkey!" The donkey observed them with pricked ears.

"Is that what was making the horrible row?" Jamie asked.

"Of course," said Natty. "Let's say hello." But as they approached, the donkey backed off.

"Careful," said Natty. "We've frightened it."

She idled to the gate and leaned over.

"Hello, donkey. What are you hee-haw honking about? Come closer and I'll tickle your ears."

"It might not want its ears tickled," said Jamie. "So watch out!"

"It will. Pebbles likes it. Penelope Potter's always getting me to tickle

Pebbles's ears. She says you can never tickle enough for him."

"But he's a pony," Jamie pointed out. "Not the same thing at all."

The donkey sniffed towards Natty's outstretched hand. Ever so gently, Natty stroked the soft nose and then worked her way up to the two floppy grey ears. As soon as she started tickling Natty knew she was right. The donkey loved it.

"There, he's leaning into my fingers just like Pebbles."

"That's not a he, that's Dora!"

Startled by this unexpected voice, they turned to find a little old lady in a flowery apron peering at them through round spectacles. She was carrying a bucket. "This is what Dora's after. Her tea. You can give it to her if you like."

"Yes, please," said Natty and took the offered bucket.

Inside were carrot peelings and a smattering of cabbage stalks. Dora gave another ear-splitting hee-haw and Natty quickly pushed the bucket under her nose. The donkey started crunching at once.

"Peace at last," said the little old lady with a smile. "I'm Mrs Jolly. Now who might you two be?"

"I'm Jamie and this is my sister, Natty," replied Jamie. "We're staying at Sea View Cottage."

"On holiday then," said Mrs Jolly. "You've got the weather for it."

Dora crunched the last of the peelings and licked the bottom of the bucket, making sure not a scrap was left.

"That was quick," said Natty.

"When it comes to eating, Dora's not one to waste time," said Mrs Jolly. "When it comes to working, that's a different matter."

"What sort of work does Dora do?" Natty asked.

"Not a lot these days," said Mrs Jolly. "She's a bit long in the tooth and creaky like me. But when she was younger she'd give donkey rides on the beach. She's too old for that now though, aren't you gal?" Mrs Jolly put out a frail hand and patted Dora's nose. "It's a pity you don't earn your keep no more, Dora, but there it is. We gets by."

Natty stroked Dora's neck comfortingly. "I expect you miss giving donkey rides, don't you Dora?"

Mrs Jolly broke into a spluttery laugh. "Dora, miss work! She'd try every trick not to go, wouldn't you gal? Talk about stubborn! Mind you, once she got started she was as good as gold. Course, now she's too old for beach rides it's hard to make ends meet. But the money has to be found. I still got to pay for Dora's winter hay. So nowadays, I takes in lodgers." Mrs Jolly tut-tutted. "I got a right pair of grumblers staying at the moment. Never stop bickering at one another, they do. Filled the old barn with all kinds of junk, they have. But they pays in advance so I'll say no more about it." Mrs Jolly held out her hand for the bucket.

"The hens is laying well. If your mum wants eggs tell her I got plenty."

They watched the old lady go back into the house and shoo out two speckled brown chickens who trotted across the yard clucking crossly. Then, with a wave, she shut the front door.

Jamie tapped his head. "Dotty," he said. "She lets chickens in the house!"

"No, she's not dotty," said Natty. "But she's very poor. She didn't even give Dora a whole carrot, just peelings and bits of cabbage stalk -

and her clothes are faded and worn."

Natty gave Dora's ears one last tickle and the donkey watched from the gate as they started back along the track. Jamie picked up a pebble and held it on his palm. He waved his other hand above it and the pebble vanished. He put the pebble back and did the same again.

"At least we know where the track goes to," said Natty, who was used to her brother making things disappear. "And I like Mrs Jolly and Dora."

Jamie tossed the pebble. "If she's got a barn and a field, once upon a time Mrs Jolly's place must have been a farm."

"I hope she lets me feed Dora again. I'll bring her lots of whole carrots," said Natty. "Another good reason for doubling my money at the magic show."

"You wish! Dad says it's a gimmick to get people to come," said Jamie, making the pebble vanish one last time.

"That's what he thinks," said Natty, when from round the bend in front of them came an old green van, bouncing chaotically in and out of the ruts. "I don't think they'd say it if it wasn't true."

"Watch out!" said Jamie, giving Natty a push. Without slowing, the van drove straight between them. The driver's face was expressionless but his passenger laughed and the van disappeared in a cloud of dust. "Of all the stupid, idiotic, crazy things!"

Natty tugged at Jamie's arm. "You know who they were, don't you? The men at the station. The ones who glued up the magic show posters."

They turned back to look, creeping through the settling dust. The van had stopped outside Mrs Jolly's house. The driver went straight in the front door and they saw the passenger disappear inside the old barn carrying a bucket.

"They must be Mrs Jolly's lodgers," said Jamie. "And if they're the fantastic Stevenage Brothers, we could get their autographs."

"I don't know about that," said Natty doubtfully, turning back for home. "Do magicians stick up their own posters?"

Jamie followed reluctantly. "We could ask them."

"But they're not very friendly. They wouldn't have cared if they'd run us over."

"No," said Jamie. "You're right, better leave it then."

Turning in the gate at Sea View Cottage, they met Dad coming down the path.

"And where did you two disappear to?" he asked.

"We found a farmhouse and met an old lady called Mrs Jolly," explained Natty. "She lives down the track and she's got a donkey called Dora."

"Ah, making friends."

"Mrs Jolly's got speckledy chickens and said to tell Mum she sells eggs. I gave Dora her tea."

"Well, you're just in time for your own tea. I was on my way to look for you."

"Great, I'm starving," said Jamie, hurrying indoors.

Neither of them mentioned Mrs Jolly's lodgers and nearly being run over by their van. Natty saved it up to tell Ned after tea. She didn't want him to miss anything exciting. Perhaps tomorrow, on their first proper day of holiday, his magic would work and he would come out of his poster.

Chapter 4
Tickets

When Natty woke the next morning, she was delighted to see Ned's poster was empty. Now all she had to do was find Ned. He was not in her bedroom, at least not as his big self. Esmerelda, Prince and Percy stood alone on the window-sill so, in between pulling on her clothes,

Natty searched the floor. Unable to find him, she looked out into the garden.

If Ned had magicked himself small he could easily have jumped through the open window. From the roof, to the wall, to the garden would be easy leaping for him. It was going to be difficult to find a miniature pony amongst so many shrubs and flowers.

He might be anywhere exploring in the early morning sunshine but, in spite of this, Natty hurried from her bedroom to try and find him. Outside in the garden, she peered between rose bushes and around tall hollyhocks, searching all the way down the path until she reached the fence at the end.

"Good morning, Natty." The voice was so unexpected she nearly jumped out of her skin.

"Ned!" she cried as a handsome chestnut pony leaned over the fence and wobbled his lips at her.

"I'm glad you didn't leave my poster behind. It's fun to be on holiday. A breath of sea air will make my magic stronger, no doubt at all." He sniffed the air. "And we're in for a splendid fine day."

Natty was thinking how wonderful it would be to jump on Ned's back and gallop to the beach, but she couldn't ignore Dad calling her from the house.

"Off you trot," said Ned. "You have your breakfast and I'll have a snack of this luscious grass, then afterwards we can go for a ride."

"Yes, please," cried Natty, flinging her arms about the pony's neck. "I'll be as quick as anything."

After breakfast, Natty was hurrying to the back door when Jamie caught her up in the hall.

"Hang on," he said. "Dad says

you're not to go off on your own. I'm coming too."

Natty's heart sank. "But. . ."

"You are going to explore, aren't you?"

"Sort of."

"Well, come on then. What are you waiting for? We'll go along the cliff path."

Natty did a quick think. She didn't want to disappoint Ned or make Jamie suspicious.

"Hang on a tick. I'll fetch my rucksack and my purse in case I want to buy something."

Natty guessed Ned would

understand her problem the moment he saw her with Jamie. With luck, Ned would magic himself tiny so she could give him a ride in her rucksack and bring him, too.

Soon Jamie was leading the way along the path towards the cliff edge. Natty stopped by the field to find it disappointingly empty. She could only hope that Ned would catch up with them.

She needn't have worried, for as the path led them through the trees, warm air and something prickly tickled the back of her neck. She knew it was Ned's whiskers, but when she turned round he had gone. Somewhere, a tiny chestnut pony was trotting through the undergrowth.

She caught up with Jamie where the path came out of the trees and forked in different directions.

"That way goes along the cliff top," said Jamie, pointing. From the corner of her eye, Natty caught sight of the tiny Ned trotting behind a thistle. "And this way takes us down to the town. I vote we walk on the pier. It's miles long."

"That's the Palace Theatre at the

end," said Natty. "Where the magic show's going to be."

"I know," cried Jamie. "We've got to look at that!" And he charged down the path.

Natty quickly took this opportunity to slip off her rucksack and unzip the front pocket.

"Thank you, Natty," cried the tiny pony and, with a flying leap, he jumped inside.

Once her rucksack was on her back Natty hurried after Jamie. Below them, Westsands spread out along the bay. Far out at sea, fishing boats dotted the water – but most impressive of all was the pier standing tall above the sands and the gently breaking waves.

"Are you all right, Ned?" whispered Natty, looking over her shoulder. She could just see Ned's head leaning out from the pocket.

"Don't worry about me. I've got a really good view from up here and I can easily hide if I want to."

"I'm giving you a ride for a change and you're as light as a feather." Then, with a little laugh, Natty hurried down the path after her brother.

They arrived at the bottom of the cliff to discover they had reached the main road. The beach lay ahead and Natty made straight for it.

"Walking in sand takes ages, Natty. Stick to the road."

"You go on. I want to go down by the sea."

"OK. Meet you at the pier," said Jamie and set off at a run.

"Now's our chance, Ned," said Natty.

"Indeed it is," said the pony. "Fancy a gallop?"

"Who's going to do the galloping, you or me?"

Ned snorted. "Me, of course. I'm the pony."

Natty peeped round to make sure no one was looking. It only took a second for the tiny Ned to leap from the rucksack and land, a Pebbles-size pony, wearing a saddle, and bridle, ready for her to mount. She took hold of the reins and swung herself on to his back. The moment she touched the saddle she was dressed in her magic riding clothes, while her rucksack became saddle-bags lying across Ned's back. This was even more exciting than her dream.

"And remember, if Jamie sees you, don't panic," said Ned. "You're wearing the perfect disguise."

Natty adjusted the chinstrap of her velvet hard hat and patted the top.

"I look completely different even though I feel exactly the same," she said. "That's what I have to remember."

"Exactly," said Ned.

The beach was deserted which was just what they needed. Ned trotted towards the firmer sand near the water's edge where he could gallop with ease.

"Hold tight," he cried.

They set off at a cracking pace with Ned's pounding feet leaving a trail of hoofprints for the tide to wash away. The wind whistled, making Natty's eyes stream tears. She crouched in her stirrups and clung on. It wasn't until they galloped under the massive iron girders of the pier that she realized how far and how fast they had come, but Ned didn't stop. He galloped on and on. She looked behind them and already the pier seemed miles away. It was breathtaking.

At last Ned slowed to a canter and turning, set off again, with an energetic bound which surprised Natty, as he had already come so far and so fast. The drumming hooves beat against the sand and the pier came closer again, until the great girders loomed above them, wrapping the pony and rider in a giant shadow.

Ned splashed into the breaking waves, his sides heaving with effort, his nostrils flaring. Here below the waterline, where the seaweed hung from the girders in limp strands, he slowed to a trot.

"Goodness, Ned, that was speedy," puffed Natty. "I don't think we've ever been that fast before."

Ned pawed at the sea, sending up salty spray to cool his tummy.

"Time for you to get off," he said, coming out of the water.

Natty checked that no one could see them and jumped to the ground. She let go of the reins and in a flash was back in her trainers, leggings and sweatshirt.

The magic wind brushed her cheek and the tiny Ned was suddenly in front of her tossing his head and bucking. She quickly pulled off her rucksack and opened the front pocket letting him jump in for a well-earned rest. Then, hoisting the rucksack on to her back, she trudged up the beach.

To her surprise, quite a crowd had gathered outside the pier entrance, with more and more people arriving to join it. Natty couldn't see Jamie anywhere and wondered why there were so many people jostling and pushing.

"Natty, over here. Quick." She was so hemmed in it took her a moment or two to realize that it was Jamie calling her.

"Natty, I'm in the queue." She pushed and wriggled her way between the crowd until it parted to reveal him at last.

"Whatever's going on?" she asked. "Why do all these people want to go on the pier?"

"They don't. They want tickets for the magic show tonight. If we don't buy them now we won't get any. That's why I'm queuing."

They moved forwards a few steps.

"Did you bring your money?" Natty asked.

Jamie looked at her anxiously. "No, but you did, didn't you?"

Natty felt in her pocket for her purse. "But will I have enough?" The queue shuffled forward a few more steps and Natty saw they were nearly at the front.

"It's lucky I got in the line when I did," said Jamie. "I wasn't sure you'd make it before they sold out."

The woman in front of them moved away and left them next at the box-office window.

"Two for the Stevenage Brothers, please," said Jamie.

The man behind the grill slammed down two tickets on to the counter.

"Ten pounds," he said.

"You'll have to pay me back," said Natty, pulling out her only ten pound note. Apart from three pound coins it was all of her holiday money gone. She handed the man the money and Jamie scooped up the tickets.

"That's it, ladies and gents. Sold out for the Stevenage Brothers." And he pulled down a blind which said Box Office Closed. There were shouts of dismay from the people standing behind them.

"Quick," said Jamie. "Let's get out of here." And he took hold of Natty's arm, pushing her through the crowd. "We've just been incredibly lucky."

"I should say so," said Natty. "Except that now I don't have much money left to double."

"It's OK," said Jamie. "Dad said he'd pay for the tickets."

Natty grinned. "That's great. In that case let's use some of what's left to buy an ice-cream at Bertollini's Ice-Cream Parlour."

"We can eat them on the pier," said Jamie, shoving the tickets into his zip pocket. "It's only twenty pence each for a pier ticket!"

Chapter 5
The Lost Bank Note

They crossed the sea front road at the pelican crossing and stopped at the pink and white shop which was Bertollini's Ice-Cream Parlour. A man, Mr Bertollini Natty presumed, was serving ice-creams from a window to customers on the pavement. He wore a straw hat with a pink band, a pink and white striped shirt and was laughing non-stop.

When it was their turn at the window he looked down at them and beamed.

"Ah ha! I have the new customer. Pretty girler, handsome boyer. You comer for your holidays?"

Natty nodded shyly. "We arrived yesterday."

"Welcome to the seasider! And now you comer to Alfredo Bertollini for ice-creamer. How you know I seller the bester in all the Westsands, eh?"

"The taxi lady said so," said Natty.

Mr Bertollini flung his arms in the air. "That lady my friender for lifer!" Then, smacking his hands together, he pointed to a picture of a magnificent ice-cream cornet.

"You want Alfredo Specials?" Natty nodded. "Good choicer. They named after me, Alfredo Bertollini!"

"How much is an Alfredo Special?" asked Natty, getting a little anxious about price.

"To youer, fifty pence each ice-creamer because I give you special offer for first tryer."

"Thank you very much," said

Natty, smiling in astonishment at this extraordinary man.

"Proper pricer one pounder. See, you getter the bargain. You eat ice-creamer here?"

"No," said Jamie. "We're going on the pier."

"So, you maker sure you don't getter loster."

"Lost where?" asked Natty.

"In the Haller of the Mirrors!" Mr Bertollini's eyes twinkled and he lowered his voice. "Everyone go in the Haller of the Mirrors and they grow fatter, and they grow thinner, and they grow taller, and they grow shorter and then they finder they can'ter get outer. What happen? They go nuts!" Jamie looked at Mr Bertollini as if he was nuts. "You don't believer? You wait till you tryer." Then Mr Bertollini caught sight of Natty's startled face. "What they don'ter know is – you gotter shout HELPer! Big louder voicer. That bringer the rescuers running."

Mr Bertollini handed them each an ice-cream exactly like the one in the picture. Having read what it said underneath Natty knew she now held an Alfredo Special Whipped Cornet with Chocolate Flake.

"And don't misser Madame LeClary's Famouser Waxworks," chuckled Mr Bertollini wickedly. "Remember Alfredo Bertollini and his deliiiicious ice-creamer and you have nicer surpriser. You see me!"

Natty put a pound coin on the counter. "Thank you, Mr Bertollini."

"You welcome. Enjoy your Alfredo Specials. My owner invention. More scrumptioso than anything you ever taster? Yeeees?"

Natty licked a large blob from her cone and her eyes lit up.

"Yes!" she said. "More scrumptioso

than anything ever!"

Jamie raised his cone in thanks. "Yummy!" he grinned.

"I glader you liker," said Mr Bertollini and, taking off his hat, he bowed low. Some people at one of the pavement tables applauded and, being in a hurry to get on the pier, Jamie pulled Natty towards the crossing before Mr Bertollini got started on something else.

"That was nice of him," said Natty. "I like Mr Bertollini and I especially like his ice-cream."

"Do you suppose he really is foreign or was he putting on that accent?"

"Oh, proper foreign," said Natty, who, in spite of going all hot and pink when the customers had applauded, had found Mr Bertollini quite charming.

"We've got to try this Hall of Mirrors," said Jamie, as the pelican went green and they crossed the road.

"Sounds a bit scary," said Natty, putting out her tongue to catch a creamy drip. On the other hand, it might offer the chance to give Ned a lick of her Alfredo Special, and Madame LeClary's Waxworks sounded intriguing.

They arrived in front of the ticket kiosk at the pier entrance to find a lady, so stout that she only just fitted behind the glass window. She was counting stitches on a long knitting needle and didn't look up. Natty put down a pound coin.

"Two halves, please."

"A hundred and twenty-seven, a hundred and twenty-eight. Increase one. Two halves coming up!" There was a double clunk and two purple tickets fell on to the silver counter. The lady counted out the change and Natty scooped it into her purse. "Push on through the turnstile and don't forget your tickets," ordered the lady and carried on counting.

They soon stepped from the concrete of the shore on to the wooden boards of the pier. It was wide enough between the cracks to see the beach below.

"Scary," said Natty, taking a big bite from her cone. The ice-cream was nearly all gone, and at this rate she didn't think Ned was going to get any. She would share Dora's carrots with him instead. "It's a long way to fall."

"Don't be daft," said Jamie. "You'd have to be a beetle to fall between those cracks." And he set off down the pier. Glancing back over her shoulder, Natty saw a pair of heavy black iron gates swing slowly open. She walked backwards, eyes on stalks, as the battered green van belonging to Mrs Jolly's lodgers motored through the pier entrance.

"Jamie," she shouted. "Look who it is!"

The van waited while one of the men closed the gates. It didn't take him long and he was soon back in his seat slamming the door. There was a gust of wind and a piece of paper blew from under the van and bounced across the decking towards Natty.

She jumped on it, saving it from the next gust which would have blown it between the railings and high over the beach. It would probably have landed on someone in a deckchair or spread flat on a towel. There were lots of people down there now. Natty picked up the piece of paper as the van drove by.

She stuffed the last of the ice-cream cone in her mouth and stared at what she held.

The paper said, Bank of England – I Promise To Pay The Bearer On Demand The Sum Of Twenty Pounds, and there was a picture of Queen Elizabeth II. Natty smoothed the creases out.

"What have you found?" Jamie asked, joining her.

"A twenty pound note! It blew from under the van. Did you see them – Mrs Jolly's lodgers?"

"You bet. They've driven right down to the end of the pier. I'm certain they're the Stevenage Brothers on their way to the theatre."

"Maybe," said Natty. She waved

the twenty pound note. "But what am I going to do with this?"

"We'll have to find out who it belongs to. You could ask this lady."

Walking towards them from the pier entrance was a lady in a straw hat carrying a newspaper.

"She wasn't anywhere near when the wind blew." But as there was no one else about, Natty decided to ask her anyway. "Excuse me, please, have you lost a twenty pound note?"

The woman slid her sunglasses down her nose and peered over

them.

"No, I don't think I have. But if you've found one you could hand it in to the lady at the turnstile or take it to the police station. Or," she said, giving this some thought, "you could spend it on ice-creams!" She pushed her sunglasses back up her nose and waited.

"No!" said Natty, shaking her head. "I couldn't do that. It's not mine."

"I'm very glad to hear it," said the lady. "Neither could I. I think taking it to the police station is the best idea. If I come across anyone who's lost a twenty pound note I'll tell them where to find it."

"Thank you," said Natty.

"Well, she wasn't much help," said Jamie when the woman was out of hearing.

"Yes, she was. We're going to take it to the police station. I'm sure Mr Bertollini will tell us where it is."

"No, wait Natty. If we go now we'll have to pay to come back again. We can go after we've seen the Hall of Mirrors and the Waxworks and maybe more of the lodgers. We've got to get our money's worth."

"OK, you can look after it then. Zip it up in your jacket pocket. You never know, we might still find out whose it is."

Jamie took the twenty pound note. "It's a nice crispy new one. I bet whoever's lost it is pretty fed up." He folded it in half, slid it into his pocket with the theatre tickets and pulled the zipper. "There, quite safe. Hall of Mirrors next. Race you."

Chapter 6
The Hall of Mirrors

It was a long run to the end of the pier and they quickly overtook the lady with the straw hat and the newspaper.

"I thought you were going to the police station," she called after them.

"We are," called Natty, turning

back. "Only we don't want to pay for pier tickets again so we're getting our money's worth first." Hoping the lady believed her, Natty raced to catch up Jamie.

It was exciting nearing the end of the pier and seeing how it opened out to make room for the great dome of the Palace Theatre and the lesser buildings on either side. There was the Hall of Mirrors, Madam LeClary's Famous French Waxworks and a place called the Burlington Arcade which Natty noticed was full of fruit machines.

Now all that could be seen

between the railings were the rolling green waves pressing forwards towards the distant shore. Men and boys lined the pier's sides with their fishing rods, hoping for a good catch. One boy had caught a crab which scuttled across the decking. Natty watched its long fall back into the sea.

Ignoring all this, Jamie reached the grand entrance to the Palace Theatre.

"It's big," he called. "Must be able to get hundreds in here and in the dark all the bulbs on the outside will light it up." Jamie tried one of the doors but it was locked.

"I wish we could look inside," he said. "Never mind. The Hall of Mirrors is open."

Natty stared wistfully at Madame LeClary's Famous French Waxworks. After what she had heard about getting lost in the Hall of Mirrors she thought finding a Mr Bertollini look-alike in the waxworks sounded a much better idea. It would have to be one or the other. Her money was running out.

Following Jamie, Natty had just reached the entrance to the Hall of Mirrors when from around the side of the theatre came

Mrs Jolly's lodgers arguing loudly.

"You have the brains of a clodhopping pea," said the one who drove the van. He prodded the other man's shoulder.

"Get off," said the prodded one. "I didn't know it was for the old biddy. I thought it was proper spending money. You could have told me it was one of ours."

"Clancy! You're so stupid. You should have recognized it, birdbrain. Anyway, losing a real one would be as bad." And he gave Clancy a shove that was so hard Natty had to jump out of the way.

"Sorry, little girl," said Clancy. "Pack it in, Rob. I nearly splatted that kid."

"Get a move on," said Rob, giving him another shove.

"Do that one more time and I won't rewire your precious tumble machine."

"You will," said Rob. "Or there'll be big trouble." But after that he left Clancy alone.

Natty hurried to Jamie's side.

"I wonder what a tumble machine is?" he asked.

Natty shook her head. "I should keep out of their way if I were you.

The one called Rob is horrible. At least the other one said sorry."

"Shan't ask for their autograph then," said Jamie with a grin.

"You still don't know they're the Stevenage Brothers," said Natty.

Jamie took her by the arm and pointed along the side of the theatre to where the battered green van was parked underneath a sign which read Stage Door. "I think they are."

"That's not proof. They could just mend tumble-driers."

"Why would repair men put up posters for a magic show?" Natty had no answer to that. "And he didn't say it was a tumble-*drier* he said it was a tumble *machine*. That's different."

"I suppose so," said Natty.

"Oh, never mind," said Jamie. "We'll do the Hall of Mirrors. I'll pay you back. Promise."

Natty glanced down the pier. The men were talking to the lady with the straw hat but Natty missed what happened next because Jamie pulled her towards the sleepy boy selling tickets for the Hall of Mirrors. The moment she paid he dropped his head on his arms. Natty didn't think he'd be much good at rescuing them if they got lost.

It was gloomy inside and, apart from them, the place was empty. They shuffled along a dark corridor until the mirrors began. After that it didn't take long before they were pulling faces and jumping up and down and turning themselves into amazing and ridiculous shapes just as Mr Bertollini had predicted.

Natty found herself short and thin in front of one mirror and tall and fat in front of another, and the expressions her face made – well, she didn't recognize herself half the time.

One minute she had giant rabbit teeth, then no teeth, then lips like balloons, then lips as thin as string. She grew ears like wings, that became droopy ears, while her eyes rounded to the size of plates. It was hilarious.

"Look at this one," cried Jamie, putting his fingers in his cheeks and pulling them wide. His teeth turned into gleaming fangs.

"Thank goodness you don't look like that all the time," grinned Natty. "I'd have to leave home." Jamie waved his head and growled.

"Don't!" Natty pushed him out of

the way and tried it herself. "Help! I look horrid!" She tried it again, pulling her lips even wider. "Jamie look!" But when she turned round he was gone. "Jamie?"

"I'm round here! This is a good one!"

But Natty couldn't see where round here was. Suddenly she was surrounded by horrible unreal people who moved in the gloom when she did.

"Jamie! Where are you? Jamie!"

She heard a shout of, "Brilliant!" but the voice was faint and she didn't know which way to go. She spun round and all the funny people spun with her.

"Steady up, Natty! I'm here!"

"Ned," she cried, half sobbing with relief. "I'd forgotten all about you."

Having jumped from the rucksack, the pony stood his full size, tacked up and ready behind her.

"Hop on," he said. "I want to have a try at this!"

Laughing with relief, Natty quickly mounted. There was a blast of magic wind and, shutting her eyes against it, she opened them to find herself trotting across a vast floor, a tiny rider on a tiny pony.

Silvered glass ribboned up for ever to a black and empty sky while the most extraordinary pony and rider appeared and disappeared in hundreds of tiny reflections. Ned cantered and reared, bowed, pawed and pranced in front of the glass at the bottom of the tall mirrors.

He came to a halt at last.

"You are the weirdest-looking pony in the whole world," laughed Natty.

"You're pretty weird-looking yourself," replied Ned, snorting and tossing his mane. "We'd better find your brother and then you can get off."

Appearing to know where he was going, he set off at a canter. Natty was thoroughly lost and left the steering to Ned. Instead, she watched the strangely contorting pony and rider leap mirrors beside them.

They found Jamie at last, disappearing up into the black sky above them, pulling another astonishing face at a reflection that was not at all like the real Jamie, but more like a giant pixie. Ned rounded a corner to allow Natty to dismount out of sight, but the sound of Rob's strident voice stopped her.

"Hey, you sonny!" he said. "We hear you found a twenty pound note. Is that right?"

Peeping out, Ned and Natty saw Rob and Clancy position themselves on either side of Jamie.

"My sister did. We're taking it to the police station."

"No need to do that," said Rob, putting on a pretend chummy voice. "It's ours. If you've got it, hand it over." With a hint of menace he leaned towards Jamie and held out his hand. Jamie stared at the stumpy fingers.

"You can claim it from the police station," he said. "If it's yours."

"Or has she got it? Your sister?" said Rob, putting his face close to Jamie's. Natty slunk down on Ned's back even though she knew Rob couldn't see her.

"You leave my sister out of it," said Jamie, leaning back to avoid him and giving an anxious glance over his shoulder.

"Don't mess me about, sonny. That money belongs to my friend here. He dropped it accidental like."

Clancy put his hand in his jacket

pocket and wiggled his fingers out through the bottom.

"I got a hole," he said. "Which I forgot."

"So it really is yours?" Jamie asked.

"That's what I'm telling you, son," said Rob, stepping back and fixing his face with a grin. "Now hand it over, there's a good boy."

"Tell you what," said Clancy, fishing in another pocket. "I'll swop it for a real—" Before he had a chance to finish his toe was stamped on. Clancy hopped around in agony.

"Just hand it over!" said Rob.

Natty could see the stubborn look grow on Jamie's face and for one awful moment she thought he wasn't going to, but at last he unzipped his pocket.

"Are you the Stevenage Brothers?" he asked.

Clancy was about to reply but clammed up when he saw Rob's warning look.

"It's none of your business," said Rob, and he snatched the note and walked off.

"It is our money, honest," said Clancy and he reached out an empty hand to Jamie's ear, pulling a

Chocolate Nobbin bar from nowhere. "Fair swop," he said, offering it.

"So you are the Stevenage Brothers," said Jamie, taking it.

A look of dismay crossed Clancy's face. He put a finger to his lips, shook his head and hurried after his brother.

"Something strange is going on here," whispered Ned.

"It is, isn't it? The sooner we find out more about it, the better," said Natty, and letting go of the reins, she jumped from Ned's back.

Chapter 7
The Real Thing

Natty longed to tell Jamie that she had seen Rob and Clancy take the money but, not wanting to give Ned away, she caught Jamie up outside the Hall of Mirrors and waited to hear all about it. Ned listened from the safety of her rucksack pocket.

"They practically forced me to give them the twenty pound note," Jamie scowled. "And anyway, how did they know we'd got it?"

"They were talking to the lady with the straw hat. She must have told them. After all, anyone losing a twenty pound note wants to find it again as fast as they can. At least, I would if I'd lost twenty pounds," said Natty. They began to walk back down the pier.

"I suppose it saves us going to the police station," grumbled Jamie. "I just don't understand why they wouldn't admit to being the

Stevenage Brothers. They should be proud to be magicians."

"But Clancy magicking the Nobbin bar was just the clue we needed. Now we know who they are! It proves you were right all along. The thing is what was Clancy going to say when Rob stamped on his foot? He'd swop it for 'a real' – what?"

"Twenty pound note, I suppose," said Jamie, snapping the chocolate bar in half and handing a piece to Natty.

"Does that mean the twenty pound note they lost wasn't real?"

"It's probably some sort of stage money for their show," said Jamie.

"If it was pretend stage money then why such a fuss to get it back? If it's pretend then it's not worth anything at all. They can't spend it, can they?"

"Of course they can't!"

"But their show's called Double Your Money! It's all a bit odd, don't you think?"

"Yes," said Jamie. "Yes, I suppose it is."

Without noticing, they reached the lady in the straw hat, who was sitting in a deckchair reading her newspaper. She looked up as they went by.

"Did the gentlemen who'd lost their money find you?" she asked, taking off her sunglasses.

Natty swung round. "Oh, yes," she replied. "Yes, they did, thank you."

"Well, that's saved you a trip to the police station. I'm glad I was able to tell them. Apparently it was part of their rent money. The chap with the hole in his pocket had forgotten to give it to their landlady. He'll be able to do that now."

"He's going to give it to his landlady?" repeated Natty.

"That's what he said," smiled the lady, slipping her sunglasses back on.

"So well done, that's your good turn for the day." She shook out her newspaper and went back to her reading.

Natty and Jamie looked at one another and hurried out of the lady's hearing.

"If it's true and the money is pretend, that's cheating Mrs Jolly," said Natty indignantly.

"Well, you saw it," said Jamie. "Did it look real?"

"I suppose so, but I've never seen a twenty pound note close up before. You saw it too, what did you think?"

"I didn't really look," confessed

Jamie. "The only thing I noticed was that it was new."

"I've got an idea," said Natty. "I'm going to ask Mr Bertollini to show me a real twenty pound note."

"And he might say 'get lost'," said Jamie.

"I shall ask all the same," said Natty, who was sure Mr Bertollini wouldn't. "I just might notice a difference."

"OK, you do that and I'll run back to the stage door and see what the Stevenage Brothers are up to. Their van's still outside."

"Be careful!" warned Natty.

"I won't let them see me. It's just to look."

While Jamie sprinted back the way they had come, Ned popped his tiny head out of the rucksack pocket.

"It's a good idea to look at a proper twenty pound note," he said. "Try and remember every bit of it."

"Yes, I will," said Natty and set off for the exit turnstile.

"So you wanter to see a real twenty pound noter?"

"Yes, please, Mr Bertollini," said Natty.

"And why, little girler, is thater?"

"Because I've never seen a real one close up before and I want to see exactly what it looks like!"

"There more reason than thiser, yes?" said Mr Bertollini. "You come into the parlour and I shower you. Then you teller me more. Angelica!" called Mr Bertollini over his shoulder. "Letter this little girler behind the counter." And he turned to serve a waiting customer.

"Thank you, Mr Bertollini," said Natty, weaving between the pavement tables to the door.

There were many more customers sitting inside the ice-cream parlour but none of them took any notice of Natty. A tall dark-haired girl lifted the counter top for her to step through. Natty smiled up at her shyly. "Hello," she said.

The girl smiled back, but before she had time to reply, Mr Bertollini pinged open the till.

"Angelica, take over the ice-creamers at the window. I shower . . . what you called little girler?"

"Natty!"

"I shower Natty the twenty pounder." With a flourish Mr Bertollini pulled out a note and handed it to her. Natty looked at it carefully. It was the same pinkie-purple colour as the other one, with a picture of the Queen and the same squiggly writing saying Bank of England but, as she moved it towards the light to get a better look, she saw something that took her by surprise.

"It's got a silver thread sewn through the middle which only shows on the front side if you hold it up to the light. How clever."

"It is," said Mr Bertollini. "The Queener Elizabeth on the fronter and Michael Faraday – famous electricity scientist – on the backer."

"I didn't look on the back of the other one."

"What other one is thater?" Mr Bertollini asked.

"The one I found on the pier," confided Natty. "I don't think it was a real one."

"Shower me. I tell you at oncer. I gotter special gadget. It checker the paper money in case I get forgery," said Mr Bertollini proudly. "I demonstrater it."

"I haven't got it any more," said Natty. "Two men on the pier said it was theirs so Jamie gave it back."

"You think it not real money but

now you can'ter prove nothing? I telephoner the police if you wanter?"

"No, don't do that," said Natty, rather startled. "I think I'd better check first, really I do."

Mr Bertollini nodded. "So, you and your brother, Jamie, you crime-bustering, are you?"

Natty shook her head and then stopped. Maybe they were crime-busting? But even if they were, it was too early to telephone the police. If the Stevenage Brothers were doing something wrong, proof was needed – and right now they had none at all. It would be terrible to make a mistake.

"Hey look!" From underneath the counter Mr Bertollini pulled a leaflet. "It say reward for helping catcher the counterfeiters. Lots of criminals at it, you see. You taker. Maybe you and your brother turn into real seasider detectives."

Mr Bertollini's eyes twinkled and, from somewhere deep in his tummy, a rumbling laugh grew until it burst from his mouth making his cheeks wobble. "Beater the crimer and I give you the freer ice-creamer," he beamed. "I, Alfredo Bertollini maker the promise."

He lifted the counter flap. Natty took the offered leaflet and went through.

"Thank you, Mr Bertollini."

"Good lucker! You need any helper, I, Alfredo Bertollini, is your man." And, still smiling, he watched Natty go out of the door.

Chapter 8
Clues

Jamie was waiting for her on the pavement. "Did you get to see one?" he asked.

"I did! I looked at it really carefully. In a real twenty pound note there's a silver strip threaded through like stitches. I don't think the one I found had that but I can't be sure. But if we got more money from the Stevenage Brothers we'd know. Mr Bertollini's got a gadget that tells real notes from forged ones. And look, he gave me this leaflet."

They read it together. *£1000 REWARD for correct information received!* it said. *Beat The Counterfeiters! Pass on what you know to the police!*

"Wow!" said Jamie. "That's a reward worth getting!"

"Better than Double Your Money any day," laughed Natty, folding up the leaflet and stuffing it in her rucksack. "What did you find out?"

"Nothing much. I saw the lodgers unload a big round drum of a thing which might be a part of their tumble machine. It had lots of wires dangling at the back and an electric motor. They took it in through the stage door. I tried sneaking in after them, but the stage door man stopped me. I guess they're setting up for their show right now."

"Well," said Natty. "If that's what they're doing, why don't we try and get some real proof that they're money forgers. We could have a look round Mrs Jolly's barn for a start."

"We mustn't get caught," said Jamie. "I don't fancy being found snooping by those two."

"You're right," said Natty. "We'll be really careful. But we can't leave town until I've bought a bag of carrots for Dora." Some were for Ned too, but she couldn't tell Jamie that. "I've just got enough money left."

A little while later, Natty was jogging along behind Jamie with her thumbs through her rucksack straps and a kilo of carrots added to her pack. She had slipped a single carrot into the rucksack pocket for Ned to chew on the way home and she hoped he wasn't being too jiggled about to eat it.

It was hot work running all the way back up to Sea View Cottage. When they reached the garden gate they stopped to get their breath back, which is where Mum found them.

"Just the people I want to see," she said, holding out two empty eggboxes. "I found these in the kitchen. Will you pop down and buy twelve eggs from Mrs Jolly for me? Here's two pounds." She gave the money to Jamie and the boxes to Natty. The children exchanged glances. They couldn't have planned it better. It gave them the perfect excuse to go down the track.

"Had a good morning exploring?" Mum asked.

"Brilliant," said Jamie. "We bought the last two tickets for the magic show!"

"And we've tried Mr Bertollini's ice-cream and been on the pier!" said Natty.

"Sounds like you've been having fun."

"We have. Especially in the Hall of Mirrors. You must go!"

"Oh, I will. But there's plenty of time." Mum turned back up the path. "Don't be too long with the eggs. It's omelettes for lunch. Then this afternoon your dad and I thought we could all go for a swim."

They set off down the rutted track for Mrs Jolly's house, listening out for the green van just in case.

"It's scary," said Natty. "What would Rob and Clancy do to us if they caught us spying?"

"No idea," said Jamie. "We must make sure they don't." Natty could tell by his tense face that he was as nervous as she was.

Knocking on Mrs Jolly's front door was the easy bit. Natty put down the egg-boxes, pulled off her rucksack and took out Dora's carrots. The donkey looked curiously at the two children over the gate.

"These are for you," Natty called, holding up the carrot bag.

When at last the door opened, Mrs Jolly peered at them, not really recognizing who they were until Natty said, "We've come for some eggs! May we have twelve, please?"

"Oh, it's Natty and Jamie," said

Mrs Jolly. "Come in, come in."

They followed the old lady into the kitchen where a black and white cat lay asleep on the table. On the window-sill by the sink was a tray of speckled brown eggs.

"Will you fill the boxes for me, Natty?" Mrs Jolly asked.

"Yes, of course," said Natty, pleased to do so. "And I've bought some carrots as a treat for Dora."

"Oh, she'll like that." Mrs Jolly put the carrot bag next to the sleeping cat.

"How much will twelve eggs be?" Jamie asked, holding out the two pounds.

"One pound twenty the dozen," said Mrs Jolly. She turned to the mantelpiece and took down a chipped blue jug, tipping the contents on to the table. There was some small change and a bundle of paper money done up with an elastic band.

"Help yourself to the right change," she said. "I can't work out those fiddly little coins even with my spectacles."

Natty's heart beat fast as she eyed the bundle of paper money. The notes were the right size and purple-

pink colour to be twenty pound ones.

"You know, I lose my lodgers today. They're leaving tonight. Not that I minds them going. Be nice to have the house to myself again. The grumble and groan lodgers I call them, but it's been worth putting up with their nonsense. They've paid me prompt and I've saved up all the rent money for the winter." And she tapped the bundle of notes with a bony finger. "Crisp new twenties, it is."

Natty turned away to the window to finish filling an egg-box. It would be the easiest thing in the world for Rob and Clancy to cheat Mrs Jolly, she realized; the old lady was so trusting and worse – short-sighted. Natty had a horrible feeling that Mrs Jolly's winter savings might prove to be worthless.

She closed the egg-box lid and watched Jamie scoop the change back into the jug and drop in the bundle of notes.

"And I won't forget to give Dora her carrots," smiled Mrs Jolly. "What a kind thought that was."

"Mrs Jolly," Natty said. "Do you mind if we have a little look round outside? A sort of explore?"

"Oh, I don't mind at all," laughed Mrs Jolly. "Just take care of them eggs."

"Thank you," said Natty. "We will." And she gave both egg-boxes to Jamie and pulled on her rucksack.

The moment they were outside and Mrs Jolly had closed the door Natty exploded. "How could those horrid Stevenages be so mean?"

"You don't know the money's forged for sure," said Jamie. "Maybe we should have asked if we could look."

"No," said Natty. "There's no point

in worrying Mrs Jolly until we're really sure it's pretend money. It's just I have this horrible feeling that it is."

"Good thinking to ask if we can look round," said Jamie, tucking the eggs out of sight behind an old stone trough. "We'll do it now while the coast is clear."

"I think the obvious place to look is in the barn," said Natty. She strode round to the big barn entrance to find the doors fastened together with a shiny brass padlock and chain. They couldn't get in.

Chapter 9
Barn Search

Dora was looking over the gate as if to say *You only had to ask me and I could have told you the barn was locked.* Natty rattled the padlock crossly. It was obvious the old doors would break before the padlock did. Jamie peered between one of the gaps near the ground where the wood had rotted but couldn't see a thing.

"It's suspicious that they've locked it," said Natty. "I want to find out what's in there."

"It might be Mrs Jolly who keeps it locked," said Jamie, disappearing round the side. "Hey, there's a window here."

"Where?" cried Natty, darting after him.

Jamie rubbed the glass with his sleeve. "It's difficult to see in."

They peered through the grimy pane and could just make out the roof beams and what might have been a workbench underneath the window.

"This is really annoying," said Natty. "I want to get inside."

Jamie lost interest once he realized

the window wouldn't open and wandered on round the end of the barn out of sight. Natty looked over her shoulder to see Ned's tiny head leaning out over the rucksack pocket.

"I think it would be a good idea to go inside, too," said the pony, and he jumped into the air. The magic wind ruffled Natty's hair and she stepped back to make space for the big Ned who suddenly stood before her. "Hop on," he said.

"Great," said Natty excitedly and, understanding at once what he was going to do, she sprang on to his back, allowing the whirling magic to spin them both tiny. Ned galloped flat out to where the barn doors stretched high above them and the padlock and chain hung impossibly out of reach.

Natty grinned, for that didn't matter now, and ducked as Ned took them through one of the gaps where the wood had flaked away, making it their own special doorway into the barn. The dust rose and a sudden beam of sunlight shone through the window, making a vast pool in the middle of the floor. They galloped by a towering wheelbarrow and the prongs of a mighty pitchfork. Jumping a coil of old rope and skirting the edge of the sunlit pool, they aimed for the enormous workbench under the window.

Ned stopped and the magic wind blew, blinding Natty until she suddenly found herself looking down on the bench instead of up at it.

"Well," said Ned, now they were big again. "What have we got here?"

"Nothing much at all," said Natty, disappointed. The bench was covered with an old bedspread. "Why keep the barn locked if there's nothing in it that's worth anything?"

Ned tossed his head. "Look under the bedspread, there might be something there."

She jumped to the ground and let go of the reins, hardly noticing her riding clothes vanish.

"There's something underneath the bench," she said, pulling the bedspread away to reveal an old brown suitcase. Testing its weight, she tried to lift it, but it was too heavy.

"Whatever's in it?"

"Open it," said Ned. "Go on. While you've got the chance."

Natty struggled to undo the catches, but it was no good; they were locked. She let out an exasperated sigh, stopping when Dora started hee-haw honking.

"What's up? It's not Dora's feeding time, is it?"

Ned pricked his ears at the door.

"It's them," he said. "Cover everything up quickly."

The chain on the door rattled.

"Get a move on, Clancy. We haven't got all day." The lodgers were right outside.

Natty grabbed the bedspread and flung it higgledy-piggledy back over the workbench.

"Get on," said Ned, but there was no time. Instead Natty raced across the barn and wriggled between some straw bales just as the doors were pulled open, while Ned went from big to small in a flash. The two brothers were silhouetted against the light and Natty hardly dared breathe in case she rustled the straw.

"Right," said Rob. "We'll check the suitcase one last time."

Desperate to look, she inched her way round the bale and saw the bedspread slide to the floor before either of the men touched it.

"How did you get it to do that, Rob?" asked Clancy.

"I didn't." Rob looked round the barn suspiciously.

"Well, there's no one else in here," said Clancy. "Can't be, the doors were locked. Must have been the wind."

"What wind?" Rob asked. "There isn't any. Most likely you not covering everything up properly."

"I did!"

"Oh, yeah, you and whose army." Rob lifted the suitcase on to the workbench. "Lovely, lovely money," he cooed, fitting a key into the lock. Clancy rubbed his hands together and Rob lifted the lid.

Natty strained to see. Then, as if it wanted to help her, the sun came out and shone another beam through the window, flooding the contents of the suitcase. Natty almost gasped – it was full of purple-pink twenty pound notes.

"Look at that," said Rob. "A sight for sore eyes."

"Yeah, lovely," said Clancy. "Lovely, lovely money." He took out a note and held it up to the light.

"Yummy, scrummy money. Lovely, yummy, scrummy money. Lovely, bubbly, yummy, scrummy BRAND NEW MONEY!"

"All right, all right, that's enough," said Rob, snatching the note and putting it back. "Now we've, how shall I put it, fabricated it. . ."

"That's a long word, Rob."

"Yeah, but it's obvious what it means, thick head." Clancy scowled behind his back, trying to work out what it did mean. "Now we've got the money prepared. That better for your brain?"

"Yes, Rob."

"If we play our cards right, by the end of tonight, we'll be rich as kings." Rob slammed down the lid and did up the catches.

"Rich," nodded Clancy, smiling now. "I like the sound of that."

"Don't bother locking the doors. Put the padlock and chain in the van. We ain't coming back here no more."

Then, picking up the suitcase, Rob carried it from the barn. Natty ducked out of sight as Clancy rolled up the bedspread and followed him.

"Lovely, lovely money, I made it carefully," he sang. "Lovely, lovely money, it all belongs to me!"

"SHUT UP!" bellowed Rob. "And get in the van."

Natty crept from her hiding-place and, keeping to the shadows, watched Rob load the suitcase before getting in the driver's seat. He drove off with a roar, leaving a trail of smelly exhaust fumes. She looked round for Ned.

"How did you get in here?" Jamie asked, suddenly arriving in the doorway and making her jump.

"Did they see you?" Natty asked.

"No. Did you get a look at what was in the suitcase? It looked incredibly heavy."

"Twenty pound notes," she said, spying her rucksack near the bench. She found Ned safely tucked inside the front pocket and pulled it on. "I can't understand why they've got so much money. They say they're going to be rich. If that money was real then they already are rich. If it's not real then what are they going to do with it?"

"Maybe we should just go to the police station and tell what we know," said Jamie.

"No! We must be sure of getting the reward. We'll have to solve the mystery ourselves, and then, if Mrs

Jolly's money is counterfeit, we can give her the reward for Dora's winter hay."

"What, all of it?"

"There'll be enough for us too, I expect."

"There'd better be," said Jamie. "But first we'll have to steal one of their twenties and Mr Bertollini must test it. Or we could ask Mrs Jolly for one of hers."

Natty shook her head. "We don't know for sure that Mrs Jolly's notes all came from the Stevenage Brothers. We need to get one from the suitcase. We'll get one tonight at the theatre when we go to the show. First we'll find out what they're up to and then go to the police."

"That's all very well to say," said Jamie. "But how will we do it?"

"I don't know quite how yet," said Natty. "But the pretend money must have something to do with their 'Double Your Money' act thing."

"We're taking a bit of a chance, aren't we?" said Jamie. "I mean, what happens if we fail?"

"We won't," said Natty. "I know we won't. We're going to catch them red-handed."

Jamie suddenly laughed. "It would be brilliant if we did. We'd be real seaside detectives, just like Mr Bertollini said." And he retrieved the egg-box from behind the stone trough.

"Yes," agreed Natty. "Seaside detectives is what we will be. I'm sure of it."

"Hee-haw!" cried Dora over the gate, as if she was sure of it too.

Besides, Natty knew what Jamie didn't; that they had Ned and his magic on their side, and Ned wouldn't let them down.

Chapter 10
Detectives on the Move

It wasn't until much later that Natty had time to have a proper talk with Ned. She'd carried him up to her bedroom the moment they'd got home, but what with being called down straight away to eat fresh egg omelettes and then going on to the beach with Mum and Dad for a swim, there had not been a minute to spare.

When at last she arrived home at the end of the afternoon she raced upstairs. She found Ned on the window-sill dozing next to Percy.

"I'm so glad you haven't gone back in your poster," she said, delighted to see him.

"I'm enjoying the view and the sea air," the pony replied. "Did you enjoy your swim?"

"I did, but I kept wondering what the Stevenage Brothers plan to do with all that money."

"Yes," said Ned. "It's a puzzler.

But don't worry, we'll find out."

Feet pounded up the stairs and they heard Jamie calling. Ned leapt for his poster and Natty jumped for the bed. By the time Jamie burst into the bedroom, the pony was back in his picture again, gazing calmly out of the window, and Natty was lying down.

"I've got your money back from Dad for the theatre tickets and here's what I owe you." Jamie handed over a ten pound note and some change. Natty gave the ten pound note a long, hard look.

"It's smaller than the twenty and

a different colour but the front is exactly the same. See the silver thread?" Natty turned the note round and held it up to the light. "It shows through the back as a black band."

"It's neat," said Jamie. "Must make it difficult to copy."

"I'm pretty certain the silver thread was missing from the money I found on the pier."

With a sigh she folded the ten pound note and put it in her purse with the rest of the money.

"Mum and Dad are going to meet us after the show," said Jamie. "We've got to have solved the mystery by then."

Natty gazed wistfully at Ned in his poster. "I wish it was time to go. When you're waiting for something to happen it takes for ever to get to the beginning."

Jamie grinned. "Know what you mean. I'm going to practise some magic tricks to fill in the time."

Natty couldn't think of anything else to do but wait.

"Be ready to go by a quarter to seven. It starts at seven-thirty, don't forget?"

"How could I?" she said.

When Jamie had gone she lay back on her bed. She wished she could work out what the Stevenage Brothers were planning. It must be some kind of pretend magic like the sort Jamie did. Jamie used sleight of hand to make things appear and disappear, or specially made tricks he bought from Cosby's Magic Emporium. That was the sort of magic Natty expected the Stevenage Brothers to do. Not real magic like Ned's.

She got up and ran her fingers across the smooth paper of his picture.

"Don't forget to be ready by a quarter to seven," she whispered. "I need your help!"

When at last it was time to go, Ned was still in his poster. Natty stood with the rucksack at the ready while Jamie's impatient shouts came up the stairs.

"Please hurry, Ned, or I'll have to go without you."

Then, before her very eyes, the pony faded from the picture and a faint breeze fluttered the paper. From nowhere a miniature pony landed on the window-sill, bucking and leaping.

"You're back," Natty cried with relief.

"Of course!" said Ned. "I wouldn't miss this magic show for anything." And, with a well-aimed jump, he disappeared into the front pocket of the rucksack. Natty gathered him up and raced downstairs.

"Come on," called Jamie. "What have you been doing!"

Dad ruffled his hair. "There's lots of time. Don't panic!"

Mum and Dad had decided to eat ice-creams at Mr Bertollini's Ice-Cream Parlour while the show was on, which was a good place to meet

Natty and Jamie afterwards.

"It's not a race," said Mum, surprised at how fast her children were walking. "You're going to be there in plenty of time."

"We want to be there in plenty of time," said Jamie, keeping up the speed until they arrived at the pier entrance.

"Enjoy the show," said Mum, who was quite puffed.

"Enjoy your ice-creams," cried Natty, giving a brief wave. Jamie showed their tickets and they hurried through the turnstile, leaving their parents behind on the pavement.

Dodging between the other people meandering along, they arrived at last in front of the open doors of the Palace Theatre. Inside, Natty glimpsed the plush red carpet and golden walls of the foyer before Jamie grabbed her arm and pulled her round the side of the building towards the stage door.

"You've got to keep the stage door man talking and I'll make a rush for it," he said.

"No," said Natty. "That's no good at all. We've got to get backstage with nobody noticing. If there's any sort of alarm we'll never get what we want."

She pulled him back towards the front of the theatre, but not before noticing the familiar green van parked under the stage door sign.

"Well, how else are we going to get backstage?" grumbled Jamie.

"I don't know," said Natty. "But not that way."

She let go of his arm and they went into the foyer. Jamie showed their tickets and an attendant directed them up the steps towards the sign saying Stalls.

"Tickets please," said another young man.

Jamie handed them over and half

was torn off. Then they were able to carry on along another red and gold corridor. To the side was a large door that led into the auditorium. Natty could see the rows of seats, but at the end of the corridor was a plain brown door marked Private which she found far more interesting.

"Shall we find our seats first?" asked Jamie.

"Later," said Natty. "I want to try the door marked Private. It leads in just the right direction for backstage."

Chapter 11
The Magic Show

Natty could see that Jamie was nervous and, if she hadn't known Ned was in her rucksack, she would have been too. As it was, she felt excited.

"How long have we got before the show starts?"

Jamie looked at his watch. "About twelve minutes."

"I'm going through that door. You keep watch. Here, give me my ticket. If I'm not back when it begins, take your seat."

Before Jamie had a chance to argue, she pushed at the door and was in luck. It should have been locked but someone hadn't pulled it shut properly. She was through in a moment, clicking up the latch to keep it unlocked ready for a quick return. She glimpsed Jamie's pale face and grinned. He tried grinning back but was too anxious to manage it. Then she closed the door and was immediately swallowed up by a wall of darkness.

"Ned," she whispered. "I think I'm backstage."

"I think you are too," came the small voice of the tiny Ned from her rucksack. "Give your eyes a chance to adjust. You'll be able to see in a minute."

Slowly, Natty moved forwards, holding her hands out in front of her in case she bumped into something. She stopped when she felt the softness of a curtain and peeped round it into the dim light ahead.

"Ned, it's the stage," she whispered. "There's a table, a cupboard and a box. They must be for the show." She moved on round until she could see the big red and gold curtain at the front of the stage closing off the audience. From beyond it came the expectant murmur of the people filling up the auditorium. The back of the stage was covered by a sweep of black curtain and more black drapes hung at the sides.

Hearing footsteps, she froze and listened to the swish of a door opening which made the curtain billow.

"Oh, there you are!" The voice belonged to a man so close she hardly dared breathe – although the curtain was between them. "This is your five minute call, gents." Natty didn't recognize him either.

"Thank you our fine stage manager, we're here and ready to go." That was Rob being pretend jolly; Natty recognized him without difficulty. "I'm going to put this suitcase here by our tumble machine and no one's to touch it. Understood?" So the tumble machine was behind the curtain too.

"No problem, Mr Stevenage. There's only me here on stage anyway. I know you magicians have your secrets."

"We do indeed, my good man," said Rob. "Clancy, stop getting under my feet."

"Sorry, Rob."

"And get a move on."

Natty slunk into the deepest gloom to hide and watched two men walk on-stage dressed in tail coats and top hats. Their faces were painted white, their eyes black and their mouths a deep red. Although she knew it was the Stevenage

Brothers, it was impossible to tell which was Rob and which was Clancy. They began quietly checking through the items on the stage.

"Quick, Natty, now's your chance," whispered Ned, jumping from the rucksack on to her shoulder.

Natty tiptoed upstage, slipping behind the wide curtain at the back and passing a door marked *To Dressing Rooms*, which is where Rob and Clancy must have come from. Here, at the back of the stage, she discovered what could only be the tumble machine. A large, see-through drum was set into a huge, black box, the top of which stretched way above her.

She could have reached the front of the drum if she'd stood on tiptoe. Both it and the box were covered with clusters of unlit coloured light bulbs. She was even more sure this was the tumble machine when she saw the jumble of electric leads and wires coming from the back. Next to the tumble machine was a stepladder and next to the stepladder was the suitcase.

Natty darted forward and quickly tried the catches. They were locked, but something peeping from under the lid caught her eye. Unbelievably, it was the end of a twenty pound note. She was about to reach for it when the heavy tread of approaching footsteps sent her scurrying and Ned flying.

"I'm not happy leaving this suitcase here, Clancy. I think we'll have it on-stage with us. It can go under the table with the other stuff."

"Right you are, Rob."

Natty's heart pounded as she crouched behind a drape looking for Ned. Where was he? There was a slow fade up of music and she knew the show was about to start. Better to be safe in the audience than lurking here where they could be discovered...

but she was running out of time to find her seat. Missing the twenty pound note was bad enough, but she couldn't go without Ned.

She darted back towards the safety of the door, hoping Ned was doing the same. She had almost reached it when, turning for one last look, she saw a tiny chestnut pony, cantering across the floorboards towards her. She bent down to pick him up and saw he was carrying a scrap of paper between his teeth which he dropped in her palm. It fluttered in an unlikely breeze and grew until Natty recognized it as a twenty pound note.

"Ned," she gasped. "You've got it!"

"Managed it without them noticing a thing," said Ned, and he jumped to her knee, then on to her shoulder. Even in this dim light Natty could see there was no silver thread in the note.

"That proves it," she said. "The suitcase is full of counterfeit money."

"And I should think that quite soon we're going to find out what they intend to do with it," whispered back Ned, before sliding into the rucksack pocket.

Folding the note, Natty peeped into the red corridor. It was empty. The music swelled into a fanfare and she ran towards the auditorium, entering as the house lights faded and a tier of spotlights blazed upon the red and gold velvet of the big stage curtain.

The theatre was packed with a sea of expectant faces. An arm waved at her and she spotted an empty seat at the end of a row. Pulling off her rucksack, she ran for it, and found herself sitting next to Jamie just as the curtain rose.

Holding the rucksack so that Ned could see, she wriggled her bottom into the seat.

"Did you get one?" Jamie asked.

Natty nearly said, Ned did, but bit her tongue in time. She nodded. "It's pretend – just as we thought."

"What shall we do?"

"Nothing now until the interval," said Natty. "We might know what they're up to by then."

She could see Ned's head peeping from the rucksack pocket, as curious as she was. Meanwhile, in the silver light on-stage, two white-faced men stood still as statues.

"It's them," whispered Natty. Jamie nodded, already entranced by the magical effect and looking forward to what was coming next.

The audience was certainly not disappointed. One of the magicians was crumpling rainbow-coloured handkerchiefs into his hand and, with a flick of his wrist, joined them together to great applause. The other magician pulled a white dove from his hat and reached in for more, filling the stage with fluttering birds.

After that, one of the men got into a box. His head stuck out from one end and his legs from the other. Then he and the box were sawn in half, and, while his legs wiggled and his head wobbled, he was wheeled in bits around the stage before being put back together again. Natty cheered along with everyone else. It was even more astonishing when he was locked in a cupboard and pierced by swords. They were shown the criss-crossed swords inside but the man had disappeared.

"Where's he gone?" whispered Natty.

"Not far," said Jamie, knowing about these things.

The swords were pulled out, and when the door was opened for the final time, the man stepped from the cupboard to loud applause. Both magicians bowed until one of them raised his hand for silence.

"Ladies and gentlemen, thank you for being such a wonderful audience. After the interval, my brother and I invite you to join in the best of our magic. Have your ten pound notes at the ready because, yes, ladies and gentlemen, we're going to Double Your Money!"

The audience cheered and whistled and the curtain came down. Ned ducked back into the rucksack and the lights came on.

"I've got it!" said Natty, suddenly standing up. "I know what they're going to do! They're going to take the real money and somehow give out the fake money. The audience will think they've got real twenty pound notes and in the meantime Rob and Clancy will get away with hundreds of proper ten pound notes which they can spend as they like."

"And if they do," said Jamie, leaping up too, "they'll escape before the audience realize they've been tricked. Why didn't we think of it before?"

Natty thrust the pretend twenty pound note into Jamie's hand. "Run to Mr Bertollini's. Tell him, tell Mum and Dad. Get them to phone the police." Natty was already pushing through the throng on her way to the door.

"Where are you going?"

"To try and stop them, of course!"

Chapter 12
Double Your Money

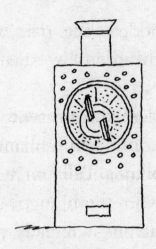

It only took Natty a moment to get backstage. There was such a crowd in the red corridor that no one saw her slip round the door. As soon as it closed behind her, Ned jumped from the rucksack and trotted ahead. She edged forwards into the gloom after him. Doing their best to keep hidden, the pair of them peeped towards the stage from behind a curtain.

The spotlights were switched off and in the dim light remaining, the faces of the conjurers were a stark and eerie white, bobbing round the tumble machine which now stood in the centre of the stage.

"Switch on, Clancy. We'll give it one final test."

Natty watched with fascination as Clancy disappeared behind the machine and clicked a switch. The coloured lights pulsed on and off as if the machine had a heartbeat. Rob pressed a silver button on the front. Natty expected the tumbled drum to revolve and was surprised when two flat paddles circled the inside instead.

Clancy appeared high above the machine and dropped some paper money into a chute on the top. It fell into the drum and was tossed into a paper storm by the paddles. A few seconds later, Rob reached between the lights and pushed down a lever. The money blew into the air from the bottom of the drum and fluttered on to the floor.

Satisfied, Rob lifted the lever back

up and pressed the silver button which switched off the paddles.

"Cover up the workings, Clancy. We've only got a couple of minutes."

Rob collected up the scattered money from the stage while Clancy set about pulling tall, black curtains around the machine, until only the drum and the bottom of the box showed. The audience would never see the chute. It was all part of the trickery.

"Clancy must have the twenty pound notes on top of the machine ready to drop into the drum," said

Ned.

"Yes," whispered Natty. "But I still don't see how they're going to swop the real money for the fake."

"We'll find out soon enough."

"But how are we going to stop them?"

"Don't worry, we will," said Ned.

Natty wasn't so confident, and hoped that by now Jamie had shown the forged note to Mum, Dad and Mr Bertollini.

"Get up your ladder, Clancy. Stand by to go."

"G-g-g-good luck!" came the nervous reply from behind the

curtain.

"This is how we get rich, mate," said Rob in a tense, excited voice. "And remember, the moment that curtain comes down we're out of here fast."

"Not half!" said Clancy.

Rob waved into the gloom on the far side of the stage. "Go music, Mr Stage Manager," he ordered, turning to face the front.

At once the music swelled, light filled the stage and the curtain rose to rousing applause.

"Ladies and gentlemen," announced Rob, raising his arms for silence and pausing for the applause and music to fade away. "This is the moment you have all been waiting for. The magical moment when you can double your money. All I ask is for one volunteer to give me a ten pound note and you will see what I can do with my Magic Money Machine."

There was more applause and cheers from the audience. Natty watched spellbound as a man came up on-stage offering a note. Rob took the ten pounds and, with a flourish, held it up for everyone to see. Next he opened a little door on the side of the drum, which Natty hadn't noticed before, and dropped it in.

He pressed the silver button and the paddles began to turn, while inside the ten pound note fluttered and twirled. A fanfare sounded and Rob pushed the lever down. A single note was blown from the machine and fluttered to the stage floor. Rob picked it up and gave it to the volunteer. The man looked at it in astonishment and held it up.

"It's a twenty," he cried. "Doubled like he said! Magic!"

The volunteer beamed happily and

took out another ten pound note. The paddles turned again and there was a gasp from the audience as another twenty pound note fluttered to the floor. The delighted volunteer clasped his doubled money and went back into the audience.

More people poured on to the stage waving ten pound notes.

"Ladies and gentlemen, there is no need to rush. This Magic Money Machine works every time. Each one of you will leave this theatre a richer person. All I need are your ten pound notes or two fives. I'm not fussy." And Rob held out his top hat to collect the money.

"This is terrible," whispered Natty. "Why don't the audience know it can't be true?"

"They think they're getting a free gift," said Ned. "They don't realize they're being fooled."

"I've got to tell them," she cried, but before Natty could rush on-stage, the magic wind blew and the big Ned blocked her way.

"They'll never believe you," he said. "Get on. There is something we can do."

Natty sprang into the saddle and at once the magic wind spun them tiny and Ned galloped for the back of the stage.

"Where are we going?" Natty cried.

"To pull the plug on that machine."

They skirted a mountainous wall of curtain and came to the bottom of the stepladder. Above them, quite out of reach, they could see the soles of Clancy's feet and, on the floor beside the steps, an open suitcase. There was a whirr from the machine, and from a slot above them a cascade of ten and five pound notes poured into it.

"Their plan's working," said Ned, looking up at Clancy. "If we don't stop them, they'll end up with hundreds and hundreds of real five and ten pound notes."

"What cheats!" fumed Natty. "They mustn't get away with it."

Clancy was working flat out, dropping fake money down the chute while more real money fell from the slot.

"Let's find that plug," cried Natty.

Ned galloped alongside the electricity lead, following it to where it plugged into a power point on the floor. The magic wind blew and they were big again. Natty slid from Ned's back, and, gripping the plug, heaved it out. There were cries of dismay from the stage as the tumble machine came to a stop and its lights went out. Natty pulled the cable as far away from the socket as she could and leapt for Ned's back enabling the magic wind to blow them tiny again.

Whimpering with fright, Clancy slid and slithered down his stepladder, scattering twenty pound notes as he went. He tested switches and pulled at knobs but to no avail.

Meanwhile, out in the audience, the uproar was growing.

"Ladies and gentlemen, we have a temporary hiccup. Normal service will be resumed as soon as possible," announced Rob, trying to calm the people who had given in their ten pound notes but hadn't yet got a twenty pound note in return. "Please, please, just give us a moment!"

Ned galloped back towards the tumble machine.

"Help, Rob!" shouted Clancy, in a complete panic, poking his head through the curtains. "I can't make it work. It's broke!"

The magic wind blew Ned big again.

"Grab the suitcase," he said, knocking the lid shut with his nose. Natty leaned over, clicked the catches shut and grabbed the handle. Before Clancy had a chance to see them, the magic wind blew again and it was a tiny pony that galloped away with its tiny rider, and an even tinier suitcase, to hide behind a curtain.

"What's going on?" the angry voices shouted. "Where's our money?"

"Bring down the curtain," shouted Rob at the stage manager, before rushing offstage. The curtain was lowered, leaving the audience buzzing angrily on the other side.

A chant of "We want our money! We want our money!" grew louder and louder.

"Quick, Ned. They're going to escape. What can we do?"

Ned spun round when four giant feet pounded by them, missing them by a whisker. He galloped in pursuit.

"Where's the suitcase with the loot?" Rob shouted.

"I don't know," said Clancy. "Gone."

Now shouts and cries came from the stage.

"Ladies and gents, please be calm and go back to your seats," cried the stage manager, trying to be heard above the uproar. Natty guessed that members of the audience must have pushed their way under the curtain.

"Leave everything," cried Rob. "Just get out of here." And he pulled open the door marked *To Dressing Rooms* and pushed Clancy through it. Natty and Ned chased after them, galloping flatout.

"They're heading for the stage

door and their van," cried Natty. "How can we stop them?"

Then, all of a sudden, Clancy was rushing back towards them yelling, "It's the police! It's the police!"

Rob came chasing after him.

"Clancy, come back! Not that way, you idiot!"

"Hold tight to the suitcase, Natty," cried Ned, and the magic wind blew. Now he filled the corridor, snorting and pawing the ground, before flattening his ears and rearing up to beat the air wildly with his front legs.

"Help! It's a mad horse! Back! Go back!" The two magicians skidded to a stop and fell over each other in their panic to run back the way they had come. Ned came down to earth again.

"Quick, get off," he said. "If the police have arrived, all is well."

Natty slid to the ground. The moment Ned was hidden in the rucksack pocket she struggled forward with the suitcase. She turned left at the end of the corridor to find four uniformed policemen holding down and handcuffing the struggling Rob and Clancy.

"Release us at once! This is an outrage," stormed Rob.

"I told you it was a daft idea," said Clancy as if he had expected to be caught all along. "That old bat can't have been as short-sighted as we thought. She must have sent the mad horse! There was a mad horse, wasn't there; or did I imagine it?"

"Shut up, big mouth," said Rob, aiming a kick.

"Well, well and what are you doing here, little girl?"

The voice came from behind her and was so unexpected it made

Natty jump. Turning round she found a friendly, freckle-faced man in ordinary clothes looking down at her and, to her delight, at his side was Jamie.

"Inspector Prince, this is my sister, Natty."

She breathed a huge sigh of relief. "Are you a real detective?"

"I am indeed," said Inspector Prince, with a reassuring smile.

"I'm glad because I've got the real money." And she offered him the suitcase.

The detective undid the catches and looked inside.

"Well done!" he said. "Thanks to you and your brother we've caught this pair of money forgers red-handed."

"It was them kids," spluttered Rob, "that found the lost twenty! I remember the boy. Clancy, this is all your fault!"

"Oh, shut up!" Clancy replied and stamped on Rob's toe, making him hop for a change.

"Take them away," ordered Inspector Prince. "And Sergeant Cork, please take this suitcase and keep it safe. It's valuable evidence and in due course the money inside it will have to be returned to its rightful owners." He smiled down at Natty and Jamie. "My next important task is to take these young persons back to their parents. Come on, my car's outside."

Chapter 13
Reward!

Inspector Prince drove them slowly down the pier, carefully avoiding all the people in the way. Natty sat with her rucksack on her lap so Ned could look out if he wanted to. The sun was sinking low across the sea and the flashing police car lights lit up the dusk, while everywhere bemused members of the audience were having their names and addresses taken.

"They'll be witnesses," said Jamie as if he knew.

"Quite right," said Inspector Prince. "And we'll be taking statements from you two as well."

"What does that mean?" Natty asked.

"You tell us the whole story and we write it down."

"Will it be a book?"

"Not a book exactly – it will be used as evidence in court to prove the Stevenage Brothers guilty."

"Does that mean we get the reward?" Natty asked, eyes alight.

"It most certainly does," smiled Inspector Prince.

"Oh, Mrs Jolly will be pleased."

"And why's that?" asked the inspector.

"We're giving her reward money to make up for all the forged notes she's been given."

"I see," said the inspector, and by the time they reached the pier entrance Inspector Prince knew all about Mrs Jolly, her lodgers, Dora and the speckledy chickens.

"That's quite a story," he said. "It'll take a lot of writing down."

The entrance to the pier was cordoned off and Mum and Dad were on the other side of the barrier, waiting.

"There they are," cried Jamie.

Natty tumbled out of the car into Dad's arms. "The forgers are caught," she said.

Dad gave her a big hug, but only after she had handed her rucksack to Jamie. The hero of the day was Ned and, although he was a secret, she didn't want him squashed!

"Well," said Inspector Prince. "Why don't we go over to the ice-cream parlour and sit down while I take a few details."

"Good idea," said Mum. "I'm looking forward to hearing a few details myself."

"These children," purred Mr Bertollini as they sat at one of his tables. "No, pardoner me, these seasider detectives catcher the forgerers? Great walnuter whips! I giver them freer ice-creamers for the rest of their stay!" He rubbed his hands with glee. "Splendiiido!"

Natty laughed. "Thank you very

much, Mr Bertollini. That will be our best reward ever, won't it Jamie?"

"How shocking this all is," said Mum.

"Not shocking no morer," said Mr Bertollini, beaming with delight. "Not now the forgerers is caught."

They licked Alfredo Special Whipped Cornets with Chocolate Flakes while Inspector Prince wrote down their holiday address and took notes. Natty told about finding the twenty pound note on the pier and Jamie about how Rob and Clancy had taken it from him in the Hall of Mirrors.

Handing out more Alfredo Specials, Mr Bertollini told how Natty had come to him to see a real twenty pound note and Natty and Jamie told of Mrs Jolly's bundle of rent money in the blue jug and how they'd been determined to get one of the notes from the suitcase.

Natty became a little fuzzy on the details of how she managed to get the forged note, not wanting to give Ned away, and Jamie relayed how he had raced down the pier to get help. Then finally Natty explained about pulling out the plug and stopping the tumble machine.

Mum and Dad sat amazed.

"You see," said Mr Bertollini. "True crime-busterers!"

"Well, I just don't know," said Mum, shaking her head. "I had no idea."

Inspector Prince closed his notebook, said a quiet "Thank you", and slipped away. After he went there were several unexpected flashes as a photographer snapped pictures of them and a young woman with a tape recorder slid into the inspector's vacant chair.

"I'm the roving reporter from the Westsands Chronicle," she smiled.

"May I do an exclusive interview?"

"You soon be famous seasider detectives. In the newspaperers, on the TVer," chuckled Mr Bertollini. "I getter more ice-creamers."

Natty looked at Jamie, wondering if she could eat another. Jamie looked stuffed full, too. They each took a deep breath, and started the story all over again.

It was very late by the time they climbed the cliff path to Sea View Cottage. A full moon shed a silver glow to show them the way and the lights of the Palace Theatre and the pier reflected on the oily dark of the sea.

"What an adventure!" sighed Natty, yawning. "I can hardly believe it happened."

Dad put his arm around her shoulder and they led the way through the woods. By the time they went in through the front door Natty was nearly asleep.

"Come on," said Mum. "Both of you upstairs to bed. Not surprisingly, after such excitement, you're worn out."

"And full of ice-cream," said Natty, who had never eaten so much in one day in her life before. She took off her rucksack and carried it up the stairs. The moment she shut her bedroom door Ned sprang on to the carpet.

"Thank you, Ned, for helping. I couldn't have done it without you."

"It's been my pleasure," said Ned, tossing his mane. "Delighted to have been of service. And tomorrow you can give Mrs Jolly the good news."

"Yes," smiled Natty. "I can hardly wait to tell her. When we get the reward she'll have plenty of real money for everything she needs.

Won't she be pleased! We'll go straight after breakfast. Will you come too?"

Ned didn't reply. A slight breeze rustled the poster and Natty saw he was a picture pony again. Slowly she undressed and pulled on her pyjamas. "Goodnight, Ned!" She climbed into bed and snuggled down. Her eyes would hardly stay open but she had one more thing to say. "Please, come back tomorrow so we can go swimming together!"

There was another rustle from the poster and Natty knew Ned had heard. With a long, satisfied sigh, she drifted into the deepest of sleeps and dreamed of presenting a delighted Mrs Jolly with a pile of reward money.

The End

Look out for more of Natty and Ned's magical adventures!

Magic Pony
Natty Saves the Day
Elizabeth Lindsay

Magic Pony
Star of the Show
Elizabeth Lindsay

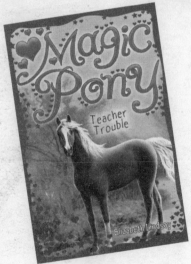

Magic Pony
Teacher Trouble
Elizabeth Lindsay